How To Propose Your Mother In Law

The Writer Ullu

Published by Dark-Community Of Owl Publishing, 2024.

HOW TO PROPOSE YOUR MOTHER IN LAW

First edition. July 18, 2024.

ISBN: 979-8227580344

Written by The Writer Ullu.

Table of Contents

Preface: Beyond the Bouquet - Building a Blossoming Bond with Your Mother-in-Law

Marriage, a joyous union, intertwines not just two hearts but two families. While the celebration overflows with shared smiles and promises, navigating the dynamics of your spouse's family can sometimes feel like deciphering a foreign language. In this intricate tapestry of in-law relationships, understanding and connecting with your mother-in-law is often the key to a harmonious extended family life.

This book isn't about getting down on one knee (although metaphorical proposals of understanding and respect are always welcome!). Instead, it's an empowering guide for building a strong, positive relationship with your spouse's mother. It's about venturing beyond the initial awkwardness and social niceties to cultivate genuine connection and mutual respect.

Here's a glimpse into what awaits you on this enriching journey:

* Decoding the Mother-in-Law Enigma: We'll delve into the complexities of the mother-in-law figure, exploring the potential anxieties and expectations that might exist on both sides. You'll gain insights into the unique perspective of your mother-in-law and discover practical strategies to build bridges of understanding.

* From Acquaintances to Allies: This book goes beyond simply tolerating your mother-in-law at family gatherings. It offers practical tools to transform your relationship into a source of support and friendship. Learn how to find common ground, initiate meaningful conversations, and foster a sense of belonging within the family unit.

* The Art of Communication: Effective communication is the cornerstone of any relationship. We'll explore strategies for active listening, respectful communication, and setting boundaries in a way that promotes harmony. You'll learn how to navigate difficult conversations and navigate misunderstandings with grace and empathy.

* Beyond the Stereotypes: We'll challenge the outdated "monster-in-law" stereotype and celebrate the diverse spectrum of mothers-in-law. You'll discover the unique qualities and wisdom each woman brings to the table and learn to appreciate their contributions to your family's life.

* The Unexpected Benefits: Building a strong bond with your mother-in-law isn't just about avoiding drama (although that's certainly a perk!). This guide unlocks the unexpected joys and benefits of a supportive in-law relationship. You'll discover a potential source of wisdom, a reliable confidante, and a partner in creating lasting family memories.

This book is for anyone seeking to navigate the wonderful and sometimes bewildering world of in-law relationships. Whether you're a newlywed facing your first family gathering or someone looking to strengthen an existing bond, this guide offers practical advice and a positive approach to building a relationship with the woman who holds a special place in your spouse's life.

Remember, creating a strong bond with your mother-in-law is an investment in your own happiness. With a little effort, empathy, and a genuine desire to connect, you can cultivate a relationship that enriches your life and strengthens your family for years to come. So, let's turn the page and embark on this rewarding journey together!

Prologue

The attic creaked underfoot, groaning with the weight of forgotten treasures. Dust motes danced in the single shaft of sunlight that pierced the gloom, illuminating a forgotten corner. There, nestled amidst cobwebbed trunks and chipped porcelain dolls, sat a dusty box. Its faded floral pattern hinted at a bygone era, and the brass clasp gleamed with a promise of secrets waiting to be unveiled.

You knelt, brushing away the years with a trembling hand. Anticipation coiled in your stomach, a blend of excitement and apprehension. This box belonged to your mother-in-law, a woman who remained an enigma despite years of shared meals and polite conversation.

Inside, nestled amidst yellowed lace and faded photographs, lay a collection of letters – a chronicle of hopes, dreams, and anxieties penned in a spidery hand. As you began to decipher the faded ink, a realization dawned. This wasn't just a box of mementos; it was a portal into your mother-in-law's heart, a window into her life before you, before marriage, before the label "mother-in-law" even existed.

With each letter, you discovered a woman beyond the social niceties. You glimpsed fears and aspirations, dreams both realized and relinquished. A picture emerged – not of a formidable figure to be appeased, but of a woman with a rich and complex history, a woman who loved fiercely and yearned for connection.

Suddenly, the awkward silences and perceived criticisms took on a new light. You understood that the path to a harmonious relationship with your mother-in-law wasn't about changing her, but about understanding her. This box, a treasure trove of memories, became the catalyst for a journey of connection, a bridge between generations, and a promise of a future filled with shared laughter and genuine understanding.

This is not simply a story about a box of memories; it's a story about the potential that lies within every in-law relationship. It's a story about venturing beyond stereotypes, about building bridges of empathy and respect, and about discovering the unexpected joys of a connection that can enrich your life in remarkable ways.

Turn the page, and let's embark on this journey together.

About D-COOP

In a literary world that often leans towards the conventional, D-COOP (Dark-Community Of Owl Publishing) emerges as a beacon for the unusual and the extraordinary. Founded by the enigmatic writer known as The Writer Ullu, this publishing house promises to redefine the boundaries of storytelling. With a name that evokes mystery and allure, D-COOP aims to be a sanctuary for unique and intriguing narratives, catering to readers who crave something different. This comprehensive exploration will delve into the origins, mission, vision, and unique qualities of D-COOP, as well as the potential impact it is poised to make on the literary landscape.

THE GENESIS OF D-COOP

The story of D-COOP begins with The Writer Ullu, a name that has become synonymous with creativity and innovation in literature. Known for their captivating stories that blend fun, facts, and the bizarre, The Writer Ullu has always pushed the boundaries of conventional storytelling. Their foray into ghostwriting added another dimension to their already diverse repertoire. However, the desire to create a platform that could house and nurture unconventional stories led to the birth of D-COOP.

The name D-COOP stands for Dark-Community Of Owl Publishing, a moniker that reflects both the mysterious and nocturnal nature of owls, as well as the collaborative spirit of a community dedicated to dark and unusual tales. This name not only captures the essence of the publishing house but also sets the tone for the kind of content it aims to produce.

MISSION AND VISION

At its core, D-COOP is driven by a mission to provide a platform for voices that often go unheard in mainstream publishing. The Writer Ullu envisioned a space where creativity could flourish without the constraints of conventional norms. The mission of D-COOP can be summarized as follows:

1. Nurturing Unconventional Narratives: D-COOP aims to publish stories that challenge the status quo, exploring themes and ideas that are often considered too unconventional for mainstream audiences. This includes everything from quirky historical facts and strange scientific phenomena to fictional stories that border on the surreal.

2. Promoting Diverse Voices: One of the primary goals of D-COOP is to amplify voices that are often marginalized or overlooked. This includes writers from diverse backgrounds, as well as those who explore themes and perspectives that are underrepresented in traditional publishing.

3. Fostering Creativity: D-COOP is committed to fostering a creative environment where writers can experiment with different styles and genres. By providing a platform for innovative storytelling, D-COOP hopes to inspire a new generation of writers and readers alike.

4. Challenging the Ordinary: In a world where much of the literature follows familiar patterns and themes, D-COOP seeks to challenge the ordinary by publishing content that is intellectually stimulating and delightfully offbeat. The goal is to offer readers a unique experience that goes beyond the typical.

THE UNIQUE QUALITIES of D-COOP

Several qualities set D-COOP apart from other publishing houses, making it a truly unique entity in the literary world:

1. Curated Content: Every piece of content published by D-COOP is carefully curated to ensure it aligns with the publishing house's mission. This means readers can expect a consistent quality and theme across all publications, whether they are reading a quirky fact book or a surreal piece of fiction.

2. Collaborative Community: D-COOP is not just a publishing house; it is a community of like-minded individuals who share a passion for the unusual and the extraordinary. This collaborative spirit is evident in the way D-COOP engages with its writers, editors, and readers, creating a sense of belonging and shared purpose.

3. Innovative Storytelling: From experimental narratives to genre-bending stories, D-COOP encourages its writers to push the boundaries of traditional storytelling. This focus on innovation ensures that every publication offers something new and exciting for readers.

4. Emphasis on Education and Entertainment: D-COOP strikes a balance between education and entertainment, providing readers with content that is both informative and engaging. Whether it's a book of strange historical facts or a fictional tale with a unique twist, readers can expect to be both entertained and enlightened.

5. Commitment to Quality: Despite its focus on unconventional content, D-COOP maintains a high standard of quality in its publications. This commitment to excellence ensures that readers receive well-crafted, thoughtfully edited content that meets the highest literary standards.

THE IMPACT OF D-COOP

The establishment of D-COOP has the potential to make a significant impact on the literary world in several ways:

1. Expanding Literary Horizons: By publishing content that challenges traditional norms, D-COOP encourages readers to expand their literary horizons and explore new genres and themes. This can lead to a more diverse and enriched reading experience.

2. Inspiring New Writers: D-COOP's emphasis on creativity and innovation can inspire new writers to experiment with their storytelling, leading to a more vibrant and dynamic literary landscape. The supportive community at D-COOP provides emerging writers with the encouragement and resources they need to succeed.

3. Amplifying Marginalized Voices: By promoting diverse voices and perspectives, D-COOP contributes to a more inclusive literary world. This not only benefits the writers themselves but also provides readers with a broader range of stories and viewpoints to explore.

4. Redefining Publishing Standards: D-COOP's commitment to quality and innovation sets a new standard for what can be achieved in publishing. Other publishing houses may be inspired to adopt similar practices, leading to a more dynamic and diverse literary industry.

THE JOURNEY AHEAD

As D-COOP continues to grow and evolve, its future holds immense promise. The Writer Ullu's vision for a publishing house that embraces the strange and unusual is already resonating with readers and writers alike. The journey ahead will undoubtedly be filled with exciting new stories, innovative ideas, and a continued commitment to pushing the boundaries of traditional publishing.

The potential impact of D-COOP is not limited to the literary world alone. By fostering a community of creative thinkers and promoting a culture of curiosity and exploration, D-COOP can inspire broader societal change. In a world that often values conformity, D-COOP stands as a testament to the power of individuality and the importance of celebrating the unique and the unconventional.

D-COOP CONCLUSION

D-COOP, the Dark-Community Of Owl Publishing, is more than just a publishing house; it is a movement. Founded by the enigmatic The Writer Ullu, D-COOP is dedicated to nurturing unconventional narratives, promoting diverse voices, and fostering a creative community. With its innovative approach to storytelling and commitment to quality, D-COOP is poised to make a significant impact on the literary world.

As it continues to grow, D-COOP will undoubtedly inspire readers and writers to embrace the strange and the extraordinary, challenging the ordinary and redefining what is possible in literature. For those who crave something different, D-COOP offers a gateway to a world of wonder and imagination, where the only limit is the extent of one's creativity.

Introduction: Unveiling the Unexpected - Building a Blossoming Bond with Your Mother-in-Law

Marriage, a symphony of joy and commitment, blends not just two lives, but two families. While the initial celebration is filled with shared promises and vibrant colors, navigating the dynamics of your spouse's family can sometimes feel like deciphering a cryptic code. In this intricate web of in-law relationships, understanding and connecting with your mother-in-law is often the key to unlocking a harmonious and fulfilling extended family life.

This book isn't about getting down on one knee with a ring for your mother-in-law (although metaphorical gestures of respect and understanding are always welcome!). Instead, it's an empowering guide, a roadmap for building a strong, positive relationship with the woman who raised the love of your life. It's about venturing beyond the initial awkwardness and social niceties to cultivate genuine connection and mutual respect.

HERE'S A TASTE OF THE enriching journey you're about to embark on:

* Unraveling the Enigma: We'll delve into the complexities of the mother-in-law figure, exploring the potential anxieties and expectations that might exist on both sides. You'll gain insights into your mother-in-law's unique perspective and discover practical strategies to build bridges of understanding.

* From Acquaintances to Allies: This book goes beyond simply tolerating your mother-in-law at family gatherings. It offers practical tools to transform your relationship into a source of unwavering support and even friendship. Learn how to find

common ground, initiate meaningful conversations, and foster a sense of belonging within the larger family unit.

* The Art of Conversation: Effective communication is the cornerstone of any relationship. We'll equip you with the tools for active listening, respectful communication, and setting boundaries in a way that promotes harmony. You'll learn how to navigate difficult conversations and navigate misunderstandings with grace and empathy.

* Beyond Stereotypes: We'll challenge the outdated "monster-in-law" stereotype and celebrate the diverse spectrum of mothers-in-law. You'll discover the unique qualities and wisdom each woman brings to the table and learn to appreciate their contributions to your family's life.

* The Unexpected Treasures: Building a strong bond with your mother-in-law isn't just about avoiding drama (although that's certainly a bonus!). This guide unlocks the unexpected joys and benefits of a supportive in-law relationship. You'll discover a potential source of wisdom, a reliable confidante, and a partner in creating lasting family memories.

This book is your compass for navigating the wonderful and sometimes bewildering world of in-law relationships. Whether you're a newlywed facing your first family gathering or someone looking to strengthen an existing bond, this guide offers practical advice and a positive approach to building a relationship with the woman who holds a special place in your spouse's life.

Remember, creating a strong bond with your mother-in-law is an investment in your own happiness. With a little effort, empathy, and a genuine desire to connect, you can cultivate a relationship that enriches your life and strengthens your family for years to come. So, let's turn the page and embark on this rewarding journey together!

Chapter 1:
Introduction to the Mother-in-Law

Part 1: Who is a mother-in-law?

A mother-in-law, also known as a mother-in-law, is the mother of your spouse. She is the woman who gave birth to the person you love dearly, the one you want to spend the rest of your life with. But let's be honest, she can also be a force to be reckoned with.

Think of her as a dragon guarding her precious treasure – your spouse. She's the gatekeeper of family traditions, the keeper of secrets, and the ultimate judge of your worthiness. So, if you're thinking of marrying her son or daughter, you better be prepared to face the dragon.

But fear not, brave adventurer! There are ways to tame this mythical beast and even turn her into an ally. With a little understanding, patience, and a whole lot of humor, you can navigate the treacherous waters of your relationship with your mother-in-law and emerge victorious.

So, who exactly is this mother-in-law creature?

Well, she can be anyone from a sweet and caring woman to a formidable force of nature. She could be a helicopter parent who still thinks her child is a baby, or a critical perfectionist who never seems to be satisfied. She could be a gossipmonger who knows everyone's business, or a social butterfly who loves to be the center of attention.

No matter what type of mother-in-law you have, one thing is for sure: she is a unique and complex individual with her own set of quirks, habits, and opinions. And if you want to have a harmonious relationship with her, you need to understand and respect her for who she is.

Here are some things to keep in mind when dealing with your mother-in-law:

She is not your mother. This may seem obvious, but it's an important distinction to make. Your mother raised you and shaped you into the person you are today. Your mother-in-law, on the other hand, is just trying to get to know you. So, don't expect her to treat you like her own child.

She has her own history and experiences. Your mother-in-law has lived a long life and has a wealth of knowledge and wisdom to share. Take the time to listen to her stories and learn from her experiences. You might be surprised at what you learn.

She loves her child very much. Your spouse is her precious child, and she wants what's best for them. So, if she seems a little protective or critical of you, it's because she's just trying to make sure her child is happy.

She is not the enemy. It's easy to see your mother-in-law as a rival for your spouse's affection, but that's not the case. She wants you to be happy with her child just as much as you do. So, try to see her as an ally rather than an adversary.

With a little effort, you can build a strong and lasting relationship with your mother-in-law. She can be a valuable source of support, advice, and love. So, don't be afraid to reach out and connect with her. You might just be surprised at how much you have in common.

Remember, the key to a happy relationship with your mother-in-law is to approach her with an open mind and a sense of humor. Don't take things too personally, and always be willing to compromise. With a little effort, you can turn this mythical beast into a lifelong friend.

Now, let's move on to the different types of mother-in-laws you might encounter in your quest for marital bliss.

STAY TUNED FOR MORE roasting and funny adventures in the next part of "How To Propose Your Mother-in-Law"!

Part 2: The Different Types of Mother-in-Laws

Ah, the mother-in-law. She's a creature of many forms, each with her own unique brand of...well, let's just say "personality." So buckle up, son-in-law (or daughter-in-law to be!), because we're about to embark on a hilarious safari through the jungle of mother-in-law stereotypes.

1. THE OVERPROTECTIVE Mama Bear

This mother-in-law sees her child as a precious cub, forever vulnerable to the harsh realities of the world (which apparently include you). She'll question your every move, from your job to your taste in socks, convinced you're one bad decision away from ruining her child's life.

* Warning Signs: She calls you for daily check-ins, subtly (or not-so-subtly) fishes for dirt on your past, and refers to your spouse as "my baby" even though they're pushing 40.

* How to Survive: Develop a thick skin, offer reassurances (but don't overdo it), and gently remind her that her child is a grown adult (hopefully).

2. THE COMPETITIVE Alpha Dog

This mother-in-law sees you as an intruder, a threat to her position as the most important woman in her child's life. She'll try to one-up you at every turn, from cooking to cleaning to unsolicited advice-giving.

* Warning Signs: She constantly compares you to her (usually exaggerated) accomplishments, fishes for compliments on her youthful looks, and passive-aggressively criticizes your cooking (especially if it's her signature dish).

* How to Survive: Don't fall into the trap of competition. Play to your strengths, and find ways to compliment her genuinely. Remember, there's room for two queens in this castle (as long as you get the bigger throne).

3. THE MEDDLING MATCHMAKER

This mother-in-law has a never-ending rolodex of potential spouses for her child, completely oblivious to the fact that they're already happily engaged (to you). Brace yourself for awkward blind dates and "accidental" meetings with her neighbor's single niece.

* Warning Signs: She guilt-trips you about not giving her grandchildren yet, expresses disappointment that you met her child "out of order" (because apparently there was a queue?), and sets you up on "friendly lunches" with random acquaintances.

* How to Survive: Maintain a united front with your spouse. Humor her suggestions (within reason), and gently remind her that your love story is already written.

4. THE GHOST

This mother-in-law is a rare breed. She's practically a myth. She's uninvolved, uninterested in your life, and perfectly content to let you and your spouse live happily ever after.

* Warning Signs: You haven't met her yet, your spouse never mentions her, and your mailbox is overflowing with wedding gifts from a mysterious "Mrs. X."

* How to Survive: Consider yourself lucky! Just be prepared to answer questions about this enigmatic figure from overly curious relatives at family gatherings.

5. THE FREELOADER

This mother-in-law sees your home as a free hotel and your wallet as an extension of her own. Prepare for extended visits that mysteriously coincide with bill-paying season.

* Warning Signs: Her luggage mysteriously expands during visits, she "forgets" her wallet everywhere she goes, and suddenly needs "financial help" for a variety of questionable emergencies.

* How to Survive: Set boundaries early on. Have honest conversations about finances with your spouse, and don't be afraid to say no to extended visits (especially if they coincide with bill-paying season).

Remember, these are just stereotypes, and your mother-in-law may be a unique blend of several types. The important thing is to approach her with humor, understanding, and maybe a few well-placed bribes (just kidding... mostly).

IN THE NEXT PART OF "How To Propose Your Mother-in-Law," we'll delve into the common challenges faced by sons-in-law and how to navigate them with grace (and maybe a little bit of trickery). Stay tuned!

Part 3: Common Challenges Faced by Sons-in-Law (and How to Survive Them)

So you've identified your mother-in-law's archetype (or maybe she's a terrifying blend of all of them). Now, let's get down to the nitty-gritty: the common challenges faced by sons-in-law and how to approach them with humor and, hopefully, emerge victorious.

CHALLENGE #1: THE NEVER-Ending Scrutiny

* The Situation: You can practically hear the judgmental gears turning in her head as you walk in the door. Her gaze flicks from your haircut to your shoes, silently critiquing your every sartorial choice.

* How to Survive: Develop a thick skin and a sense of humor. When you catch her appraising stare, give her a playful wink and say, "Looking good today, yourself, Mrs. [Spouse's Last Name]." Defuse the tension with a little lightheartedness.

CHALLENGE #2: THE COMPETITIVE Cooking Contest

* The Situation: Every dinner at her place is a culinary battlefield. Her mashed potatoes are the creamiest, her gravy the smoothest, and woe betide you if you dare compliment a dish that isn't hers.

* How to Survive: Team up! Offer to help in the kitchen and learn her secret recipes. Then, shower her with praise and declare that you could never compete with a master like her. A little flattery goes a long way.

CHALLENGE #3: THE HOLIDAY Gift Gauntlet

* The Situation: The holidays become a stressful game of gift-giving one-upmanship. No matter how thoughtful your present, it somehow pales in comparison to her extravagant offerings.

* How to Survive: Focus on experiences over expensive gifts. Plan a weekend getaway for you and your spouse, or offer to take her on a fun outing. It'll show you put thought into the gift while staying within your budget.

CHALLENGE #4: THE ENDLESS Stream of Advice (Solicited or Not)

* The Situation: She has an opinion on everything, from your career choices to your living room decor. And she's not shy about sharing it, whether you want to hear it or not.

* How to Survive: Thank her for her input, then politely explain that you and your spouse will make the final decision. You can also try deflecting with humor. "Wow, that's a great idea, Mrs. [Spouse's Last Name]! We'll have to add it to the suggestion box."

CHALLENGE #5: THE HUSBAND Stealing

* The Situation: She still refers to your spouse as "my baby" and subtly tries to pull them back into the nest. Weekend visits mysteriously turn into month-long stays, and inside jokes only they understand fly back and forth.

* How to Survive: Maintain a united front with your spouse. Plan fun activities together that include your spouse's mom, gently reminding her that you two are a team now.

Remember, communication is key. Talk to your spouse about your concerns, and work together to navigate these challenges. A little effort and a lot of humor can go a long way in building a strong relationship with your mother-in-law.

IN THE NEXT PART OF "How To Propose Your Mother-in-Law," we'll explore the importance of a good relationship with your mother-in-law and the benefits it can bring. Stay tuned!

Part 4: The Importance of a Good Relationship with Your Mother-in-Law

Let's face it, a good relationship with your mother-in-law can feel like winning the lottery. She can be a source of love, support, and even unexpected wisdom (gasp!). Here's why having her on your side is a win-win situation:

* Built-in Babysitting: Need a night out? Your mother-in-law might be thrilled to spend quality time with her grandkids, giving you and your spouse some much-needed couple time.

* Unbiased Advice (Sometimes): Believe it or not, your mother-in-law can offer a different perspective on things, having known your spouse for, well, their entire life. Her advice might be blunt, but it could be honest and valuable.

* A Partner in Crime (for Good): Maybe you both share a love for cheesy reality TV or a talent for embarrassing your spouse with childhood stories. Having your mother-in-law as your partner in crime can create hilarious memories and a special bond.

* A Wealth of Family History: She's a living archive of your spouse's family history. Those embarrassing childhood photos? She's got them all. But seriously, learning about your spouse's roots can bring you closer to them and give you a better understanding of who they are.

* A Fierce Defender: Mess with you, mess with her. A good mother-in-law will have your back through thick and thin, becoming a formidable ally against anyone who tries to come between you and your spouse.

* Reduced Stress: Let's be honest, a strained relationship with your mother-in-law can be a major source of stress. Building a positive connection can eliminate that tension and create a more peaceful home environment.

SO, HOW DO YOU GO ABOUT achieving this marital nirvana? Here are some tips:

* Show genuine interest in her life. Ask her questions about her hobbies, her past, and her dreams.

* Include her in family activities and outings. Make her feel like a valued member of the family.

* Offer help and support when you can. This could be anything from fixing a leaky faucet to running errands.

* Be respectful and communicate openly. Even if you disagree, do so with kindness and understanding.

* Find common ground. Maybe you both love cooking or a particular genre of music. Bond over shared interests.

Remember, building a good relationship takes time and effort. But the rewards are worth it. A supportive mother-in-law can become a lifelong friend and confidante. So, put down your defenses, pick up your sense of humor, and who knows, you might just find yourself enjoying your mother-in-law's company!

This concludes Chapter 1 of "How To Propose Your Mother-in-Law." In the next chapter, we'll delve into the fascinating world of understanding your mother-in-law, her personality, and her unique perspective. Get ready for some psychological insights and, of course, more laughs!

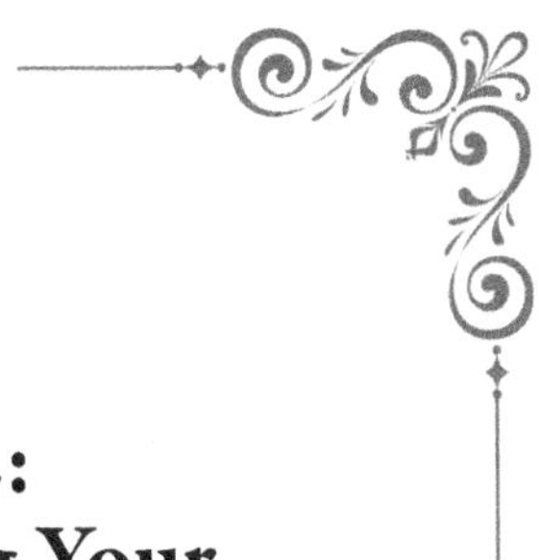

Chapter 2:
Understanding Your
Mother-in-Law

Part 1: Personality and Interests

Ah, the mother-in-law. An enigma wrapped in a mystery inside an enigma... or maybe she's just a woman with a rich tapestry of experiences and quirks. Regardless, understanding her personality and interests is the key to unlocking a harmonious relationship. So, grab your magnifying glass, son-in-law (or daughter-in-law to be!), because we're about to dissect the fascinating psyche of your spouse's mother.

* The Myers-Briggs Approach:

Sure, you could take a wild guess at her personality type based on her social media posts (endless cat videos? Introverted!), but why not get a little more scientific? The Myers-Briggs Type Indicator (MBTI) can offer valuable insights into her preferences and motivations. Is she an ISTJ, the stoic and practical planner? Or perhaps an ESFP, the social butterfly who thrives on excitement? Understanding her MBTI type can help you navigate conversations and avoid stepping on any toes.

* Beyond the Labels:

Remember, MBTI is just a starting point. Don't get hung up on labels. Observe her behavior in different situations. Does she light up at a lively party or find solace in a quiet corner with a good book? These subtle cues can tell you a lot about her introverted or extroverted tendencies.

* Hobby Hunting:

What makes her tick? Does she spend her weekends gardening or conquering crossword puzzles? Take an interest in her hobbies. It's a great way to bond and discover shared passions. Who knows, maybe you'll find yourself enjoying a relaxing afternoon of birdwatching with your mother-in-law (hey, it could happen!).

* The Power of Observation:

Pay attention to the little things. Does she have a prized collection of porcelain dolls or a bookshelf overflowing with self-help manuals? These seemingly insignificant details can reveal a lot about her values and interests.

Remember, understanding your mother-in-law's personality and interests is a journey, not a destination. By putting in the effort, you can build a stronger connection and create a more peaceful coexistence.

In the next part of "How To Propose Your Mother-in-Law" (yes, you read that right, propose!), we'll delve into her background and family history. Get ready for some surprising revelations and maybe a few skeletons in the closet (hopefully not literally).

Part 2: Background and Family History

So you've gotten a glimpse into your mother-in-law's personality and interests. Now, let's delve even deeper into her fascinating backstory. Unraveling her family history is like embarking on a historical adventure, filled with twists, turns, and maybe even a few scandals (hopefully not too many). Here's why knowing her past is key to understanding your present:

* The Root of Her Beliefs: Her upbringing, cultural background, and life experiences have shaped who she is today. Understanding these factors can help you see the world through her eyes and appreciate her perspective.

* Explaining the Quirks: Does she have a weird obsession with polka dots or a deep-seated fear of clowns? There's probably a story behind it! Her childhood experiences or family traditions might hold the key to these seemingly random quirks.

* Building Bridges, Not Walls: Knowing about past family feuds or cultural clashes can help you avoid sensitive topics and navigate conversations more smoothly.

* Unearthing Hidden Gems: You might discover shared ancestry or surprising connections to historical events. Who knows, you could find out your families were neighbors back in the day!

* Finding Common Ground: Maybe her grandfather was a famous jazz musician, or her family immigrated from the same country as yours. These shared experiences can create unexpected bonds and strengthen your relationship.

So, how do you become an investigative biographer of your mother-in-law's life? Here are some tips:

* Engage in Casual Conversation: Ask her open-ended questions about her childhood, her parents, and her siblings. Let the conversation flow naturally and avoid grilling her.

* Dig Through the Photo Albums: Old photos can spark a treasure trove of memories. Ask her about the people in the pictures and the stories behind them.

* Family Gatherings are Goldmines: Use family reunions or holidays as opportunities to chat with her relatives. They might have interesting anecdotes about her younger days.

* Be Respectful of Boundaries: Not everyone enjoys reliving the past. If she seems uncomfortable with a particular topic, politely move on.

Remember, understanding your mother-in-law's background is a delicate dance. Be patient, respectful, and genuinely interested. The more you learn about her history, the better equipped you'll be to build a strong and lasting relationship.

In the next part of "How To Propose Your Mother-in-Law" (brace yourself!), we'll explore her values, beliefs, and expectations for you and your spouse. Get ready for some honest conversations and maybe a few compromises.

Part 3: Values, Beliefs, and Expectations

Understanding your mother-in-law's value system is crucial for navigating your relationship. Her beliefs about family, religion, money, and life in general have shaped her expectations for herself, her children, and you by extension.

DECODING HER VALUES:

* Observe her actions. How does she spend her free time? Does she volunteer at a charity or prioritize work success? These choices reflect what she values.

* Listen to her conversations. What topics does she bring up frequently? Does she emphasize honesty, compassion, or hard work?

* Engage in respectful dialogue. Ask open-ended questions about her upbringing and the values instilled in her.

BRIDGING THE GAP:

* Find common ground. You might share similar values on family or education, even if you differ on others.

* Agree to disagree. Respect her beliefs even if they don't align with yours. Open-mindedness fosters a more peaceful coexistence.

* Focus on shared goals. Perhaps you both prioritize a happy and healthy life for your spouse. This common ground can be a bridge between differing values.

MANAGING EXPECTATIONS:

* Open communication is key. Discuss your and your spouse's goals for the future. Be honest about your plans and aspirations.

* Set boundaries. If her expectations clash with your reality, have a calm conversation about what's feasible.

* Focus on the positive. Highlight how your values and goals complement hers, even if there are some differences.

Remember, your mother-in-law is an individual with her own unique perspective. By understanding her values, beliefs, and expectations, you can build a stronger relationship based on mutual respect and open communication.

In the next chapter, we'll delve into the art of building a strong bond with your mother-in-law. Get ready for practical tips and strategies for creating a harmonious relationship!

Part 4: Her Expectations for You and Your Spouse

Ah, expectations. They can be the invisible strings that bind relationships or the tangled knots that unravel them. When it comes to your mother-in-law, understanding her expectations for you and your spouse is crucial for navigating the often-choppy waters of family dynamics. Here's why:

A WINDOW INTO HER DREAMS:

Your mother-in-law likely has hopes and dreams for her child's future happiness. By understanding her expectations, you can gain valuable insight into what she values most in a partner for her son or daughter.

AVOIDING UNNECESSARY Conflict:

If you're unaware of her expectations, you might inadvertently clash with them, creating unnecessary tension in the relationship. Knowing what she expects can help you avoid stepping on any landmines.

BUILDING TRUST AND Respect:

When you demonstrate a genuine interest in her perspective, you show her respect and build trust. This paves the way for a more open and harmonious relationship.

UNPACKING THE EXPECTATIONS:

So, what kind of expectations might your mother-in-law have? It's a mixed bag, and will vary depending on her personality and background. Here are some common themes:

* Financial Stability: Does she expect you to be a high earner, or is financial security less of a concern for her?

* Family Values: Does she prioritize traditional family structures, or is she more open-minded about modern family dynamics?

* Religious Beliefs: Does she expect you to share her religious beliefs, or is she accepting of different faiths?

* Lifestyle Choices: Does she have strong opinions on your career paths, hobbies, or even where you live?

NAVIGATING THE MAZE:

Now that you have an idea of the potential expectations, how do you navigate them? Here are some tips:

* Open Communication: Talk to your spouse about your mother-in-law's potential expectations. Have honest conversations about your own goals and values as a couple.

* Set Boundaries: It's okay to set boundaries with your mother-in-law, especially if her expectations are unrealistic or controlling. Your spouse can play a crucial role in having this conversation.

* Focus on Shared Goals: Perhaps you both want a happy and stable future for your spouse. Highlight these shared goals to bridge the gap between differing expectations.

* Show Respect, Even if You Disagree: Even if you don't agree with her expectations, treat them with respect. Explain your perspective calmly and rationally.

* Focus on Your Strengths: Don't try to be someone you're not. Highlight your strengths and positive qualities as a partner for your spouse.

Remember, building a strong relationship with your mother-in-law is a marathon, not a sprint. By fostering open communication, setting boundaries, and demonstrating respect, you can create a harmonious environment where both of your needs are met.

In the next chapter, we'll finally move on from understanding your mother-in-law to the exciting part — building a strong and lasting relationship with her! Get ready for practical tips and strategies for creating a bond that goes beyond obligation.

Chapter 3: Building a Bond with Your Mother-in-Law

Part 1:
Communication and
active listening

Congratulations! You've made it through the sometimes-daunting task of understanding your mother-in-law. Now comes the fun part: building a strong and lasting relationship with her. This goes beyond simply tolerating each other at family gatherings. It's about creating a genuine connection built on mutual respect, understanding, and maybe even a shared love for reality TV (hey, it's a start!).

FROM ACQUAINTANCES to Allies:

Here are some practical tips to transform your relationship with your mother-in-law from polite acquaintances to supportive allies:

* Find Common Ground: This is the golden rule. Do you both love hiking, cooking a particular cuisine, or binge-watching historical dramas? Bonding over shared interests creates a foundation for a stronger relationship.

* The Power of Two: Plan activities that involve both you and your spouse. This can be anything from a weekend getaway

Part 2: Spending quality time together

Conquering Common Challenges: A Mother-in-Law Survival Guide

The path to a harmonious relationship with your mother-in-law isn't always smooth sailing. Here are some common challenges you might face, along with strategies to overcome them:

THE UNSOLICITED ADVICE Avalanche:

* The Tactic: Acknowledge her input with a polite "Thank you for your thoughts," then explain your approach (as a couple) and why it works for you.

* The Bonus Tip: Sometimes, a simple "We'll keep that in mind" can politely deflect unwanted advice.

THE COMPETITIVE COOKING Contest:

* The Tactic: Offer to collaborate in the kitchen! Learn a signature recipe from her and share your own culinary skills. It becomes a bonding experience, not a competition.

* The Bonus Tip: Focus on compliments. Praise her cooking genuinely and highlight the effort she puts into preparing meals.

THE GIFT-GIVING GAUNTLET:

* The Tactic: Focus on experiences over expensive gifts. Plan a fun outing together or offer to help with a project she's been putting off. It shows thoughtfulness without breaking the bank.

* The Bonus Tip: If you do go the traditional gift route, personalize it! Choose something that reflects her interests or a shared memory.

THE HOLIDAY HAVOC:

* The Tactic: Communicate openly with your spouse and come up with a plan for the holidays that works for everyone. This might involve alternating between families or creating new traditions together.

* The Bonus Tip: Offer to help out! Volunteer to host a specific meal or take on a decorating task. Sharing the workload reduces stress and fosters a sense of teamwork.

THE OVERSTEPPING BOUNDARIES Barrier:

* The Tactic: Have a calm conversation with your spouse about the boundaries you need to establish. Then, your spouse can communicate these boundaries to their mother in a respectful way.

* The Bonus Tip: Focus on "I" statements. Explain how her actions make you feel and propose solutions that respect both your needs.

Remember, communication is key! Open and honest conversations with your spouse and your mother-in-law are essential for navigating these challenges.

BUILDING A STRONG FOUNDATION:

* Team Up with Your Spouse: Present a united front. Discuss strategies together and support each other in navigating your relationship with your mother-in-law.

* Remember, It's a Two-Way Street: Put in the effort to build a relationship with her, not just the other way around. Show genuine interest in her life and make time for her.

* Celebrate the Victories (Big and Small): Acknowledge the progress you've made in your relationship. A shared laugh, a heartfelt conversation – these moments signify a growing bond.

* Patience is a Virtue: Building a strong bond takes time. Don't get discouraged if there are setbacks. Celebrate small victories and focus on consistent effort.

* Embrace the Journey: The process of building a relationship with your mother-in-law can be an enriching experience. You might learn new things about yourself and your spouse along the way.

BY APPROACHING CHALLENGES with understanding, respect, and a healthy dose of humor, you can navigate the complexities of your relationship with your mother-in-law. Who knows, you might even discover a cherished friend in the process!

In the final chapter of "How To Propose Your Mother-in-Law" (don't worry, it's not a literal proposal!), we'll explore the long-term benefits of a strong relationship with your spouse's mother. Get ready to discover the joys of having a supportive and loving extended family.

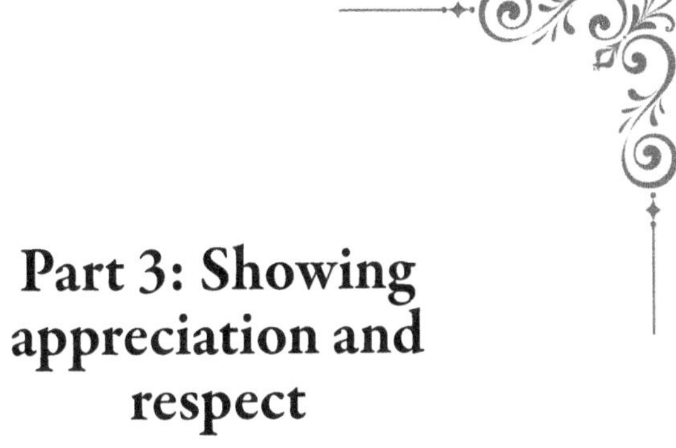

Part 3: Showing appreciation and respect

The Long-Term Rewards: A Supportive Family Unit
So you've weathered the storms, navigated the challenges, and nurtured your relationship with your mother-in-law. Now it's time to reap the rewards! Here's why having her as a trusted confidante and ally can enrich your life:

* A Built-In Support System: Life throws curveballs. Knowing you have your mother-in-law's support, whether it's emotional or practical, can be a lifesaver during challenging times.

* A Partner in Parenting (if you choose): A supportive mother-in-law can be a valuable resource when you have children. She can offer advice (solicited this time!), help with childcare, and create a loving bond with your kids.

* A Wealth of Family History and Traditions: She's a living archive of your spouse's family history and traditions. This knowledge can strengthen your connection to your spouse and enrich your family life.

* A Source of Unexpected Fun: Who knows, you might discover you share a love for karaoke nights or quirky travel

destinations. A strong bond opens doors to shared experience and unexpected adventures.

* A Friend and confidante: Over time, your relationship might blossom into a genuine friendship. You can share joys, sorrows, and silly memes, creating a special bond that goes beyond family ties.

Remember, a good relationship with your mother-in-law is a gift that keeps on giving. It strengthens your marriage, enriches your family life, and brings more love and laughter into your world.

CONGRATULATIONS! YOU'VE reached the end of "How To Propose Your Mother-in-Law" (well, almost). In the final chapter, we'll explore some bonus tips and remember, this guide isn't just about proposing... it's about proposing a lasting and positive relationship!

Part 4: Helping out and being supportive

Bonus Tips and Rememberances

We've covered a lot of ground on building a strong and rewarding relationship with your mother-in-law. Here are some final tips and reminders to keep in mind:

* Celebrate Her Wins: Be genuinely happy for her successes, big or small. A thoughtful card or a heartfelt phone call shows you care.

* Embrace Forgiveness: Everyone makes mistakes. Learn to forgive and move on. Holding onto resentment only harms the relationship.

* The Power of Humor: Laughter is a universal language. A shared laugh can ease tension and create a more positive atmosphere.

* Don't Compare: Every relationship is unique. Don't compare yours to others on social media or in movies. Focus on building your own authentic bond.

* Enjoy the Journey: Building a strong relationship takes time and effort, but it's a worthwhile pursuit. Savor the small victories and enjoy getting to know her better.

Remember, this guide isn't just about proposing a good relationship with your mother-in-law, it's about building a lasting and positive one. Your efforts will not only benefit you and your spouse but also create a more harmonious and supportive extended family.

Here's to a future filled with laughter, love, and a mother-in-law who feels more like family!

Congratulations! You've completed "How To Propose Your Mother-in-Law." While it might not involve getting down on one knee, this guide equips you with the tools and strategies to build a strong, supportive, and rewarding relationship with your spouse's mother.

Chapter 4: It's Not Just About Your Mother-in-Law: Building Strong Relationships with Your Spouse's Family

Congratulations! You've delved into the wonderful (and occasionally challenging) world of understanding and building a bond with your mother-in-law. But a strong relationship with your spouse's entire family can be just as important for creating a happy and fulfilling home life.

EXPANDING YOUR HORIZONS:

While your mother-in-law might be the first hurdle, here's how to cultivate positive connections with the rest of your spouse's family:

* Get to Know Them Individually: Just like your mother-in-law, each family member is an individual. Take the time to learn about their interests, hobbies, and dreams.

* Find Common Ground: Do you share a love for board games with your father-in-law or a passion for gardening with your sister-in-law? Bonding over shared interests strengthens connections.

* Show Genuine Interest: Ask questions, listen attentively, and remember details they share. This shows you care about their lives and experiences.

* Offer Help and Support: Is your brother-in-law struggling with a DIY project? Offer a helping hand. Small gestures demonstrate your willingness to be a supportive part of the family.

* Embrace Their Traditions: Participating in family traditions shows respect for their heritage and creates shared memories for you and your spouse.

In the next part of Chapter 4, we'll explore the beautiful rewards of cultivating strong bonds with your entire in-law family.

The Rewards of a Strong In-Law Network

Building positive relationships with your in-laws isn't just about avoiding drama (although that's a perk!). Here are some incredible benefits that come with having a supportive and loving extended family:

* A Built-In Support System: Facing a tough time? Knowing you have a network of in-laws who care about you and your spouse can be a source of immense emotional strength.

* A Village for Raising Children: It takes a village, as they say. In-laws who are actively involved in your children's lives can provide childcare support, love, and guidance, enriching your family unit.

* A Wealth of Knowledge and Experience: Your in-laws have a lifetime of experiences to share. Learn from their wisdom, whether it's about parenting advice, career tips, or simply funny family anecdotes.

* A Celebration of Diversity: In-laws from different backgrounds bring unique traditions, perspectives, and even cuisines to the table. This diversity can broaden your horizons and create a more vibrant family life.

* A Source of Unexpected Fun: Family gatherings don't have to be stressful. With strong bonds, they can be filled with laughter, shared hobbies, and the joy of creating new memories together.

Remember, investing in relationships with your in-laws is an investment in your own happiness. A supportive extended family creates a sense of belonging, strengthens your marriage, and enriches your life in countless ways.

THE FINAL CHAPTER

In the final chapter of "How To Propose Your Mother-in-Law" (figuratively speaking, of course!), we'll wrap things up with some inspirational thoughts and a reminder that building strong in-law relationships is a journey, not a destination. Get ready for a heartwarming conclusion!

Building Bridges, Not Walls: A Final Word

Congratulations! You've reached the final part of "How To Propose Your Mother-in-Law" (metaphorically, that is). Throughout this journey, we've explored the complexities and rewards of building strong relationships with your spouse's family. Remember, this is a marathon, not a sprint. There will be moments of laughter, shared experiences, and maybe even a few bumps along the road.

Here are some inspiring thoughts to keep in mind as you navigate your in-law relationships:

* Focus on the Positive: Every family has its quirks, but choose to focus on the good things. Appreciate your in-laws for their unique qualities and the love they bring to your life.

* Celebrate Small Victories: Building strong bonds takes time and effort. Acknowledge the progress you've made, no matter how small. A shared conversation, a thoughtful gesture – these all contribute to a more positive dynamic.

* The Power of Forgiveness: We all make mistakes. Learn to forgive your in-laws (and yourself) for past slights. Holding onto resentment only hinders the growth of your relationships.

* Embrace the Journey: Building a strong in-law network is an ongoing process. There will be challenges, but there will also be moments of unexpected joy and connection. Savor the journey and enjoy getting to know your extended family.

Remember, you have the power to shape the narrative of your in-law relationships. By approaching them with respect, kindness, and a genuine desire to connect, you can create a supportive and loving extended family that enriches your life in countless ways.

So, the next time you see your mother-in-law (or any in-law!), smile, take a deep breath, and remember the incredible journey you're on. You're building a future filled with love, laughter, and a strong, supportive family by your side.

Congratulations! You've completed "How To Propose Your Mother-in-Law." May this guide empower you to navigate the wonderful world of in-law relationships and create a harmonious and joyful extended family!

Chapter 5: The Unexpected Benefits of Having Awesome In-Laws

Building strong relationships with your in-laws isn't just about avoiding drama (although that's a perk!). It's about cultivating a network of supportive individuals who enrich your life in surprising ways. Here, we'll delve into the unexpected benefits of having awesome in-laws:

* The Wisdom Whisperers: Your in-laws are a treasure trove of life experiences. They've navigated careers, relationships, and countless challenges. Tap into their wisdom! Seek advice on career paths, parenting dilemmas, or even DIY home renovation projects. Their insights can be invaluable.

* The Cheerleading Squad: Life throws curveballs. Having in-laws who celebrate your successes, big or small, is a gift. They'll be there to cheer you on during a job promotion, a new creative endeavor, or even mastering that tricky recipe. Their unwavering support is a powerful motivator.

* The Built-In Babysitters: Need a night out? Awesome in-laws can be lifesavers! Knowing your children are in their loving care allows you and your spouse to relax and recharge. Bonus points if they spoil your kids rotten (within reason, of course!).

* The Cultural Connectors: In-laws from different backgrounds can introduce you to new customs, traditions, and even cuisines! Embrace the opportunity to learn about their heritage and expand your cultural horizons. These shared experiences can strengthen your bond and create lasting memories.

* The Travel Buddies (Maybe): Do your in-laws share your love for adventure? Exploring new destinations together can be a fantastic way to solidify your connection. Imagine creating travel

memories with your spouse and in-laws, forging a unique bond through shared experiences.

* The Laughter Lifeline: Sometimes, you just need a good laugh. Awesome in-laws can be a source of amusement and lightheartedness. Sharing inside jokes, reliving funny family stories, or simply enjoying their quirky sense of humor can be a wonderful stress reliever.

* The Unconditional Love Network: Family isn't always about blood. Awesome in-laws can offer a sense of belonging and unconditional love, which extends to your children as well. This creates a secure and supportive environment for your entire family unit.

Remember, the benefits of having awesome in-laws are as unique as the individuals themselves. Embrace the unexpected joys, the shared experiences, and the sense of belonging that a strong in-law network brings.

So next time you see your awesome in-laws, express your gratitude for their presence in your life. You might be surprised at the richness and joy they bring to your journey!

This concludes "How To Propose Your Mother-in-Law" (metaphorically speaking, of course!). I hope this guide empowers you to cultivate strong and rewarding relationships with your spouse's family.

Beyond the Tangible: The Emotional Riches of Strong In-Law Bonds

The benefits of having awesome in-laws extend far beyond the practicalities of childcare or travel companions. Here, we explore the emotional riches that come with cultivating strong bonds with your spouse's family:

* A Sense of Belonging: Family isn't just about who you share DNA with. It's about feeling accepted, loved, and supported. Awesome in-laws can create a sense of belonging that extends beyond your immediate nuclear family. This feeling of being part of something bigger can be incredibly grounding and comforting.

* A Bridge Between Generations: In-laws connect you to your spouse's family history and traditions. Sharing stories, photos, and cultural practices creates a bridge between generations. This connection to your spouse's roots can deepen your understanding of them and strengthen your bond as a couple.

* A Shared Legacy: As your family grows, you'll create new traditions and memories with your in-laws. These shared experiences become part of a rich family tapestry, a legacy you can pass down to future generations.

* Unwavering Support System: Life can be unpredictable. Knowing you have a network of in-laws who care about you and your spouse provides invaluable emotional support. They'll be there to celebrate your victories and offer a shoulder to cry on during tough times.

* A Source of Personal Growth: Relationships with in-laws can challenge you to see the world from a different perspective. Learning to appreciate their values and beliefs, even if they differ

from your own, can foster personal growth and broaden your horizons.

* The Gift of New Friendships: Sometimes, in-laws become close friends. Shared interests, hobbies, or simply a mutual love for your spouse can blossom into genuine friendships that enrich your life outside of family gatherings.

Remember, strong in-law relationships are a two-way street. Invest time and effort in getting to know them, be open to their perspectives, and show genuine appreciation for their presence in your life. The emotional rewards will be immeasurable.

In the final part of Chapter 5, we'll offer some practical tips for nurturing and maintaining these valuable bonds with your awesome in-laws.

Nurturing the Bond: Keeping Your In-Law Relationships Strong

You've cultivated fantastic relationships with your in-laws – that's a win! But like any relationship, it requires effort to maintain the bond. Here are some tips for keeping the connection strong:

* Schedule Regular Catch-Ups: Make time for dedicated interactions outside of family gatherings. Grab coffee with your mother-in-law, invite your father-in-law to a sporting event, or plan a game night with the whole in-law crew.

* Express Gratitude: A simple thank you for a thoughtful gesture, a heartfelt card, or a phone call expressing your appreciation go a long way. Let your in-laws know how much you value their presence in your life.

* Stay Connected (But Respect Boundaries): Regular texts, phone calls, or even video chats can keep the lines of communication open. However, respect their privacy and avoid being intrusive.

* Include Them (But Don't Force It): Invite them to participate in activities you enjoy, but don't pressure them if they decline. Respect their preferences and find ways to connect that work for everyone.

* Embrace Their Uniqueness: Awesome in-laws come in all personalities. Appreciate their quirks and differences – they add richness to your life!

* Focus on Shared Experiences: Plan activities that create lasting memories. This could be anything from a weekend getaway to a cooking class you take together.

* Maintain Open Communication: Address any issues that arise in a respectful and timely manner. Bottling up frustrations

can create distance. Clear communication builds trust and strengthens the bond.

Remember, building strong in-law relationships is a journey, not a destination. There will be bumps along the road, but with consistent effort, respect, and a genuine desire to connect, you can cultivate a network of awesome in-laws who enrich your life in countless ways.

This concludes "How To Propose Your Mother-in-Law" (metaphorically, of course!). May this guide serve as a reminder that strong in-law relationships are an investment worth making. They bring laughter, love, and a sense of belonging that extends beyond blood ties.

The Final Toast: A Celebration of Family

We've reached the final part of our journey in "How To Propose Your Mother-in-Law" (metaphorically speaking!). Throughout this exploration, we've delved into the complexities and rewards of building strong relationships with your spouse's family.

Let's raise a metaphorical toast to the concept of awesome in-laws. They are more than just relatives; they can be confidantes, cheerleaders, and cherished members of your extended family.

Here's a final thought to leave you with:

Building strong in-law relationships isn't about achieving some picture-perfect ideal. It's about fostering genuine connections, appreciating their uniqueness, and celebrating the beautiful tapestry of family that you're creating together.

Remember, you have the power to shape the narrative of your in-law relationships. By approaching them with open hearts, empathy, and a dash of humor, you can cultivate a network of love and support that enriches your life in remarkable ways.

So, the next time you see your in-laws, offer a warm smile, and remember the incredible journey you're on. You're building a future filled with love, laughter, and a strong, supportive family by your side. Cheers to that!

This concludes "How To Propose Your Mother-in-Law."

I hope this guide has empowered you to navigate the wonderful world of in-law relationships and create a harmonious and joyful extended family. You've got this!

About the Author

The Writer Ullu is a name that resonates with uniqueness and creativity in the literary world. Known for their captivating stories that blend fun, facts, and the bizarre, The Writer Ullu has carved a niche that stands out. Recently, they have ventured into the realm of ghostwriting under the same name, adding another dimension to their repertoire. Alongside this, they have founded their own publishing house, D-COOP (Dark-Community Of Owl Publishing), which promises to be a sanctuary for unconventional and intriguing narratives. The content produced by The Writer Ullu, now under the banner of D-COOP, offers readers a delightful mix of entertainment and education, often exploring the strange and unusual. This new chapter in their career not only broadens their creative horizons but also provides a platform for other voices to emerge, all while maintaining the distinctive charm and originality that defines The Writer Ullu.

Read more at www.dcoopbooks.rf.gd.